IMAGINE THAT™

Licensed exclusively to Imagine That Publishing Ltd
Tide Mill Way, Woodbridge, Suffolk, IP12 1AP, UK
www.imaginethat.com
Copyright © 2019 Imagine That Group Ltd
All rights reserved
0 2 4 6 8 9 7 5 3 1
Manufactured in China

Retold by Nat Lambert
Illustrated by Christina Forshay

ISBN 978-1-78958-448-6

A catalogue record for this book is available from the British Library

The Three Billy Goats Gruff

Illustrated by Christina Forshay

Retold by Nat Lambert

Once upon a time, there lived three Billy Goats Gruff. It was summer and the grass in their meadow had turned dry and brown, but the goats knew there was lots of tasty, fresh green grass up in the mountains, so they set off one by one on their journey.

The youngest and smallest Billy Goat Gruff was the first to reach a big stone bridge.

On the other side, he could see
fresh green grass in the distance,
so he ran ahead excitedly.

TROLL BOOTH

Clip-clop! Clip-clop! Clip-clop!

Suddenly, a troll appeared. He had scary eyes, sharp yellow teeth and horrible horns!

'Where do you think you're going?'
demanded the troll.

TROLL BOOTH

'I'm going across the river
to eat the tasty green grass!'
replied the smallest Billy Goat Gruff.

'Oh no you're not!' replied the troll.

'I'm going to **gobble** you up!'

'**Wait!**' cried the smallest Billy Goat Gruff. 'You don't want to eat me. I'm so small, you would never be full. My brother is following me. He is much bigger and tastier. You should eat him instead.'

'**Bigger** and tastier?'
said the greedy troll. 'Alright,
you can cross the bridge.'

And the smallest Billy Goat Gruff
skipped away to eat the
fresh green grass.

A little later, the middle Billy Goat Gruff arrived to cross the bridge.

Clip-clop! Clip-clop! Clip-clop!

TROLL BOOTH

Out jumped the greedy troll again.

'Stop! Where do you think you're going?'
he shouted.

'To join my brother on the other side of the river,'
replied the middle Billy Goat Gruff.

'Oh no you're not!' replied the troll.

'I'm going to gobble you up!'

'**Wait!**' cried the middle Billy Goat Gruff.
'You don't want to eat me. My hair is so long, it would get stuck
in your teeth. My brother is following me.
He is even bigger and tastier. You should eat him instead.'

'Even **bigger** and **tastier?'**

smiled the greedy troll, his stomach rumbling.
'Okay, you can cross the bridge.'

So, the middle billy goat quickly crossed
the bridge to join his brother.

Now the troll was getting really excited about eating the biggest Billy Goat Gruff. While he waited, he studied his favourite cookbook, planning exactly how he would eat him all up. Finally, he heard hooves on the bridge.

Clip-clop!

Clip-clop!

The greedy troll bounded out.

'**Where do you think you're going?**'

he roared.

'To join my brothers on the other side,'
replied the largest Billy Goat Gruff.

But as the Billy Goat Gruff got closer, the troll realised that he was the largest billy goat he had ever seen. He had two enormous horns and towered over the troll!

'You're going to gobble ME up?' laughed the largest Billy Goat Gruff.

'I don't think so!'

TROLL BOOTH

STOP

And with that, the largest Billy Goat Gruff ran towards the greedy troll and butted him right into the air.

Up, up and up flew the troll. Then down, down and down he fell until he landed in the river with an enormous

KERRSPLASH!

The largest Billy Goat Gruff snorted, then crossed the bridge to join his brothers on the other side of the river, where they ate as much tasty, fresh green grass as they wanted.
And as for the greedy troll ...

... he never bothered anyone crossing the bridge again!